Strong and P[...]

Written by Lauren Wilke
Illustrations by Lauren Wilke

This book is dedicated to Sharon and Mick, (Strong and Powerful), for giving a home to Honey Jack and Finnegan! Also, to everyone who rescues a pet, giving them a second chance at life.

First there was a mother and a teenage boy.

I guess I didn't bring them much joy.

They dropped me off, and my wait began.

I was left in this cold foreign land.

A women came by with a smile and she cried.

But then she came back, and she just sighed.

An old man who was just looking for a friend.

He found a friend at the other end.

"What was I to do?", I asked everyone with my eyes.

But the only answer I got was their sorry goodbyes.

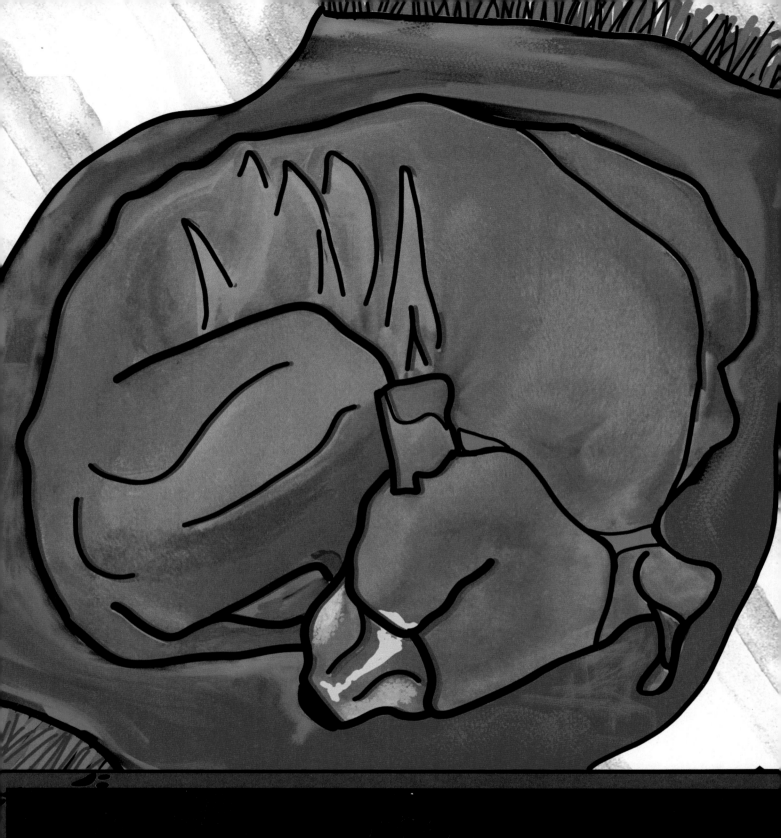

My life has been extremely hard and cold.

I think I am going to get too old.

My days are numbered while waiting in here.

Will anyone ever find me dear?

Then these two people with purpose came along.

She had purple hair and seemed very strong.

The man was powerful with a gray beard and a deep voice.

I wonder who in here will be their choice.

With serious pace they walked by once more.

With gesturing hands, they were pointing at my door.

The walker came then, and I heard my door go click.

I figured this had to be a trick.

The old blue leash hooked to the collar around my neck.

I really hoped I wasn't going for a vet check!

The sun hit my face, Strong and Powerful were waiting outside.

Maybe, possibly, is it time to turn the tide?

In the sunshine scared with my head held low and shy.

I heard myself wimper, it was my turn to cry.

Strong and powerful brought me to their warm safe home.

I never dreamed I would never be alone.

Made in the USA
Middletown, DE
15 July 2022